For Bella with all my love, from Mum

– A.P.

For my sister Jen, my real-life fire fox

– S.M.

Author's Note

This story is inspired by a Saami myth from Finnish Lapland, of the *revontulet*,
or fox fires – sparks that fly from the fur of a magical fox known as Tulikettu,
soaring into the sky to create the Northern Lights.

First published 2021 by Two Hoots
an imprint of Pan Macmillan
The Smithson, 6 Briset Street, London EC1M 5NR
EU representative: Macmillan Publishers Ireland Limited,
1st Floor, The Liffey Trust Centre,
117-126 Sheriff Street Upper, Dublin 1, D01 YC43
Associated companies throughout the world
www.panmacmillan.com
ISBN: 978-1-5290-5655-6 (HB)
ISBN: 978-1-5290-5656-3 (PB)
Text copyright © Alexandra Page 2021
Illustrations copyright © Stef Murphy 2021
Moral rights asserted.

www.twohootsbooks.com

ALEXANDRA PAGE STEF MURPHY

The FIRE FOX

TWO HOOTS

When winter came, Freya and her mum went to stay in a little log cabin.

"Your dad loved this old place," said Mum. "He used to say it was magical.

It's just what we need for a while."

But Freya didn't like it.

Everything felt cold and empty with just the two of them.

"Why don't you explore while I unpack?" Mum said. "I'll be right here."

Freya wasn't sure. But the softly falling snow did look perfect for sledging.

Freya wrapped herself up,
tugged on her boots and pulled
the sledge to the doorway.

But when she looked out, the wind shrieked, branches creaked and a cold gust blew in. Freya shivered. She was about to close the door, when she saw a strange light out on the snow.

Two golden eyes blinked and a small shape crept out of the trees. Freya gasped as she saw . . .

. . . a white fox!

His bushy tail twitched in a friendly way as he padded closer to Freya.

"Hello," she whispered, stepping outside.

The fox's fur shone like moonlight.

He darted across the snow and looked back, waiting for her.

For a moment Freya forgot her fear. She followed, keeping close the cabin.

At the edge of the trees, Freya watched as the fox began to hop from shadow to shadow. Where his paws touched the frosty ground, coloured sparks flew up from the snow.

Freya took a small jump. Snowflakes scattered in the air like stars. She smiled as they darted and dipped, sprang and skipped through the flickering forest.

Freya and the fox reached

the top of a steep slope.

The wind whistled around them.

"Where shall we go now?" Freya said.

The fox tugged the rope gently.

Freya held tight and he pulled her down
the hill, fiery lights flashing from his fur.
Freya laughed as they twisted and tipped,
swerved and slipped down the shimmering slope.

The fox ran on with Freya. His tail swished from side to side, sending frosty fires spiralling into the starlit sky.

"Let's go faster!" Freya shouted happily.

Suddenly the fox let go of the sledge.

"Come back!" Freya cried.
But soon the fox was so far away
Freya couldn't see him anymore.

Freya felt cold and empty without the fox.

Until, slowly, she felt a glow spreading

out above her. She looked up.

The sky was dancing with light!

Freya watched the fox fires flickering over the hills and trees and snow.

Not far away was the glow of the little

log cabin, where Mum was waiting.

Freya ran back to find her.

"Look Mum," Freya said. "He made it just for the two of us!"

They watched together, until the last light faded from the sky.

But Freya didn't feel cold or empty anymore.

Because inside, the light still shone.

**The item should be returned or renewed
by the last date stamped below.**

PILLGWENLLY

Dylid dychwelyd neu adnewyddu'r eitem erbyn
y dyddiad olaf sydd wedi'i stampio isod.

_____

_____ _____ _____

_____ _____ _____

_____ _____ _____

_____ _____ _____

_____ _____ _____

_____ _____ _____

_____ _____ _____

_____ _____ _____

_____ _____ _____

_____

To renew visit / Adnewyddwch ar
www.newport.gov.uk/libraries